THIS BOOK BELONGS TO

The Adventures of
Bella & Harry

Let's Visit Athens!

Written By
Lisa Manzione

Illustrated By
Kristine Lucco

Bella & Harry, LLC

www.BellaAndHarry.com
email: BellaAndHarryGo@aol.com

Today we are in Athens, Greece, enjoying the sights and sounds of this ancient city with our family.

Macedonia

Bulgaria

Albania

GREECE

Aegean
Sea

ATHENS

Mediterranean Sea

Turkey

Athens is one of the oldest cities in the entire world. The history of Athens spans over 3,000 years! Today, Athens is the largest city in Greece. It is also the capital of Greece.

First stop... The Olympic Stadium!

"Harry, did you know the very first modern Olympic Games were played in this stadium in 1896? The games were officially known as 'The Games of I Olympiad'."

"**Modern** Olympic Games, Bella?"

"Yes Harry, the first modern games were here in Athens. The ancient Olympic Games were held in another area of Greece called Olympia."

"Ancient Olympic Games, Bella?
What is the difference between the ancient Olympic Games and the modern Olympic Games of today?"

HISTORY
OF THE
OLYMPIC
GAMES

"**The** ancient Olympics were held thousands of years ago. It is thought the ancient games were mostly foot races. The games were held to honor the gods of Mount Olympus."

·20·

11

zeus was believed to be the king of the gods of ancient Greece and was very important in Greek mythology. Greek mythology is legends or stories written about ancient Greece.

"**One** day, Harry, we will read Greek mythology, but today we are in Athens having fun!"

"**Hurry!** We are off to see the Acropolis!"

"**Bella,** is that the Acropolis on the top of the hill?"

"**Yes,** Harry! The Acropolis is a religious complex that was built thousands of years ago. The most famous building in the complex is the Parthenon."

16

"**The** Parthenon was built to worship the Greek goddess Athena.
Athena was known as the goddess of wisdom.
The Temple of Athena Nike is also part of the Acropolis."

"Nike? Do you mean a Temple of Tennis Shoes, Bella?"

"Harry, you are so silly! I am not talking about Nike shoes! I am talking about the Temple of Athena Nike! Nike means victory in the Greek language. The ancient people worshiped at this temple during times of battle hoping for victory and success."

19

"Let's go Harry! We are walking to the Plaka to have an authentic Greek lunch!"

"Where is the Plaka, Bella?"

"**The** Plaka is located below the Acropolis. It is one of the oldest areas in Athens. The Plaka has fun walking areas and only a few cars are allowed. There are several restaurants to choose from. We can rest our puppy paws while our family enjoys lunch."

21

22

"It looks like the children are having a fun lunch! They are having saganaki (pan fried cheese), along with spanakopita (feta cheese and spinach wrapped in phyllo dough), moussaka (eggplant, ground beef and potato casserole) and baklava (phyllo dough, honey and walnuts) for dessert!"

23

"BELLA! BELLA!
The pan is on FIRE!"

"It's okay Harry! We are having saganaki, also called flaming cheese!"

25

Opa! Opa!

"Bella! What is that word I hear?"

"**Harry,** that is a Greek word meaning 'hooray' or 'to celebrate'! It is a fun word! Let's say it together... Opa! Opa!"

"**We** are off to the port. The port of Piraeus is the main port in Athens, and the largest port in Greece."

28

"**We** are going to take a fun, very fast ride on a high speed ferry boat from Piraeus to one of the neighboring Greek islands... Crete!"

"What's in Crete, Bella?"

"**We** are going to see the Minoan Palace of Knossos. The Palace of Knossos was a place where King Minos of Crete once lived. It is a place of legends and myths about the Minotaur and the labyrinth!"

"A Minotaur, Bella?"

"**Yes,** the Minotaur was a figure in Greek mythology. The Minotaur had the head of a bull and the body of a man. Legend says the King kept the Minotaur in the labyrinth (or maze like garden) of the Palace."

"A myth, Bella? Are you sure a myth is only a story?"

"Yes, Harry, I am sure."

"Let's go! We are heading back to the ferry boat for our ride back to Athens."

31

Well, our day of fun is over. We loved our visit to the city of Athens and the Greek islands! There is so much to see. I think we will return for another visit, but for now it's "Anti'o-sas"... or good-bye in the Greek language... from Bella Boo and Harry too! See you soon on our next adventure!

Our Adventure to Athens

Visiting The National Archaeological
Museum of Athens.

Visiting the ruins of the ancient
Olympic stadium.

The Erechtheion is a part of the
Acropolis complex.

Exploring the ruins in Athens, Greece.

Harry marching with the "Evzones", guards in the Greek army!

A fun donkey ride in Santorini! Santorini is another Greek island.

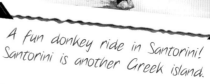

Harry posing with a painting from ancient Greece.

Looking at the beautiful sea from the island of Mykonos.

Common Greek Words and Phrases

Restaurant – Taverna

Good Morning – Kalimera

Good Evening – Kalispera

Please! – Parakalo'!

Yes – Ne

No – Ohi

Thank You! – Efharisto!

Do you speak English? – Milas Anglika?

What time is it? – Ti ora ine?

Library of Congress Cataloging-in-Publications Data is available

Manzione, Lisa

The Adventures of Bella & Harry: Let's Visit Athens!

ISBN: 978-1-937616-05-2

First Edition

Book Five of Bella & Harry Series

For further information please visit:

www.BellaAndHarry.com

or

Email: BellaAndHarryGo@aol.com

CPSIA Section 103 (a) Compliant

www.beaconstar.com/consumer

ID: L0118329. Tracking No.: L1412423

Printed in China